Disney
Robin
Hood

Robin Hood lived in Sherwood Forest. He stole from the rich and gave to the poor.

One day, Robin and his friend Little John saw King Richard's royal carriage passing by. In it was Richard's selfish brother, Prince John, who was acting as king while his brother was away. This gave Robin an idea.

Robin and Little John disguised themselves as fortunetellers and ran after the royal carriage.

When he saw the gypsies, the prince ordered his men to stop the carriage.

Robin and John brought out their crystal ball and began their act. The prince stared into the ball. He was spellbound by all the riches the fortuneteller foresaw.

Robin took gold with him as he left the carriage. Meanwhile, Little John had gathered as many coins as he could carry from a hole in the bottom of the royal chest of gold.

When he was done, Little John loosened the carriage wheels.

Prince John suddenly realized he had been tricked.

“Catch those thieves!” he hollered.

By this time, Robin and Little John were already off and running. The prince tried to follow them in his carriage, but it wasn’t long before the loosened carriage wheels fell off, bringing their chase to an end.

When he returned to the castle, the prince called on the Sheriff of Nottingham.

One of the sheriff's duties was to collect taxes. The vengeful prince happily raised taxes to punish Robin for his thievery.

The sheriff started his collection at Bobby's house.

It was Bobby's birthday and, as a gift, his sisters had given him a shiny gold coin.

When the sheriff saw the coin he took it. Thankfully, Robin arrived a few moments later and replaced Bobby's stolen coin with a bow and arrow!

Soon afterward, everyone was talking about the Golden Arrow Tournament. The best archer would be rewarded with a kiss from the lovely Maid Marian.

Robin was in love with Marian. He signed up for the tournament disguised as a stork. With a little luck, he could win Marian's kiss.

Robin was known to be the best archer in the country, so he ignored the fact that the tournament was surely a trap set up by the prince.

At the end of the day, only two archers remained: the stork and the sheriff. With his final arrow, the stork hit the bull's-eye.

Marian was thrilled. She knew that the stork was really Robin. As Robin bowed to her, Prince John tore through Robin's costume with his sword.

The sheriff threw Robin in prison.

As Prince John stood up he felt the point of a dagger in his back. It was Little John disguised as a royal court attendant.

"Let Robin go!" demanded Little John. "Otherwise..."

The prince had no choice. Robin and Little John escaped again.

The prince was furious. He raised taxes once more, and the sheriff was more than happy to collect. By the end of the day, the only gold coin that remained in the town was in the poor box. The sheriff collected the last coin without a thought.

When Friar Tuck scolded the sheriff, he was thrown in prison.

Some time later, Prince John devised a brilliant plan to capture Robin.

"I'll use Friar Tuck as bait," said the prince. "When Robin comes to free him, we'll be ready for him."

Robin disguised himself as a blind beggar and went to Prince John's castle. Fooled by his disguise, the guard let Robin in. He and Little John crept through the castle in search of the sheriff.

When Robin found the sheriff, he was sleeping soundly. He carefully stole his keys and tossed them to Little John.

"Release Friar Tuck and the other prisoners," he whispered. "I'm going to find the treasure."

The prison was full of people who hadn't paid their taxes, including Friar Tuck. Little John released them all.

In a chamber, Robin found Prince John and Sir Hiss sleeping. The prince held two bags of gold to his chest and dreamed of owning all the riches in the world. His bedroom floor was littered with bags of gold.

Robin tied a long rope to the tip of his arrow and shot it toward the spot where Little John and Friar Tuck were waiting.

He fastened the bags of gold to the rope one by one, and slid them down the line toward his friends.

As the bags slid down, Little John and Friar Tuck collected them. Suddenly a small noise woke Sir Hiss.

Robin grabbed the rope before Prince John and Sir Hiss could catch him. Robin had escaped once again!

Sir Hiss stretched out and grabbed a bag of gold in his fangs. The bag ripped, spilling coins all over the ground.

The prince screamed, waking the royal archers. They, too, joined the hunt for Robin.

Robin finally made his way down the rope and fell into Little John's arms.

Friar Tuck, Little John and the prisoners ran toward the moat, while Robin stayed behind to confront the sheriff. In the scuffle, the sheriff tripped, setting the drapes on fire.

The fire spread quickly through the castle. Robin leaped from the burning tower to escape the flames. He swam to shore and took off into Sherwood Forest.

The castle burned down and the prince was left penniless.

A few days later, church bells rang throughout the kingdom, celebrating King Richard's return. At last, peace would be restored!

Marian and Robin Hood were married and they lived happily ever after.